The Brothers Grimm

Snow-white

and other fairy tales

Miles
Kelly

First published in 2015 by Miles Kelly Publishing Ltd
Harding's Barn, Bardfield End Green, Thaxted, Essex, CM6 3PX, UK

Copyright © Miles Kelly Publishing Ltd 2015

2 4 6 8 10 9 7 5 3

Publishing Director Belinda Gallagher
Creative Director Jo Cowan
Editorial Director Rosie Neave
Designer Rob Hale
Production Elizabeth Collins, Caroline Kelly
Reprographics Stephan Davis, Jennifer Cozens, Thom Allaway
Assets Lorraine King

ISBN 978-1-78209-746-4

Printed in China

British Library Cataloguing-in-Publication Data
A catalogue record for this book is available from the British Library

ACKNOWLEDGEMENTS
The publishers would like to thank the following artists who have contributed to this book:

Front cover and all border illustrations: Louise Ellis (The Bright Agency)

Inside illustrations:
Snow-white and the Seven Dwarfs Mónica Carretero (Plum Pudding Illustration Agency)
The Gold Children Martina Peluso (Advocate-art)
The Valiant Little Tailor Polona Kosec (Advocate-art)
The Little Folks' Presents Lucia Masciullo (Pickled Ink)

Made with paper from a sustainable forest

www.mileskelly.net
info@mileskelly.net

Contents

Snow-white and the Seven Dwarfs

One winter's day, a queen sat by a window, sewing. She accidently pricked her finger with the needle, and saw how beautiful the red looked against the dark ebony window frame and the white snow.

Soon after that the queen had a baby girl. She had skin as white as snow, lips as red as blood and hair as dark as ebony. She was named 'Snow-white'.

Sadly the queen died soon after, and the king married again. His new wife was beautiful but cruel – and she was a witch. She had a magic mirror, and every day she would ask it: "Mirror, mirror, on the wall, who is the fairest of them all?"

And the magic mirror would answer: "You, O queen, are the fairest of them all."

And the queen would admire her reflection and smile.

But one day, when Snow-white was seventeen, the magic mirror replied: "You, O queen, are very fair – but Snow-white is the fairest of them all."

The queen was shocked! She couldn't bear the thought of anyone being more beautiful than her. Full of envy and hatred, she called a huntsman and told him, "Take Snow-white into the forest and kill her. Bring me her heart, as proof."

The huntsman was terrified of the evil queen, and dared not disobey. He seized

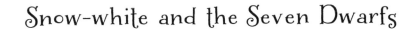

Snow-white in secret and carried her off to the forest. But he could not bring himself to kill the beautiful, weeping girl! Instead, he told her: "Run away and never come back, for the queen wants to kill you!"

The huntsman slew a young boar and took its heart back to the queen, saying he had carried out her wishes. And Snow-white disappeared through the trees, as fast as her legs could carry her.

Snow-white was so frightened that she ran and ran until evening began to fall. At last, just as the sun was setting, she stumbled across a pretty little cottage set in an opening in the trees. She was so exhausted that she knocked at the door. To her surprise, the door opened at her touch, and she crept in to rest for the night.

Everything in the cottage was small, but very neat. There was a table laid with seven little plates, seven little knives and forks and spoons, and seven little mugs. There were seven little chairs pulled up around the fireplace, and against the wall stood seven little beds. Snow-white ate a tiny bit from each plate and drank a tiny sip from each mug. Then she sank down on a tiny bed and fell fast asleep.

Later that night the owners of the cottage came back – they were seven dwarfs, who had been hard at work all day mining in the mountains for jewels. They were astonished

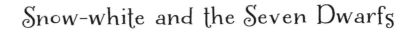

to see Snow-white. "Oh, heavens!" they cried. "Is it an angel?" The little men watched over her all night.

When Snow-white awoke, she was surprised and a little frightened to find that she was not alone. But the little men spoke kindly and gently. Snow-white explained what had happened and the dwarfs took pity on her at once. "You are very welcome to stay here with us," they invited, and the grateful girl agreed.

From then on, while the dwarfs went out to work in the mines, Snow-white looked after their cottage and cooked supper. "Beware your stepmother," the dwarfs reminded her each day. "She will find out

9

that you are not dead and come looking for you. While we are out at work, never let anyone in!"

Months went by and Snow-white was very happy. She and the dwarfs became very fond of each other. But then one day the queen stood before her magic mirror again and it told her: "You, O queen, are very fair – but Snow-white is alive, living with the dwarfs in the forest, and she is the fairest of them all."

At once the queen realized the huntsman had tricked her, and she stamped her feet with rage! Then she muttered an evil spell and made a magic apple. It looked beautiful – as though it would taste delicious – but only the green side was safe to eat, the rosy side was poisonous! Then the queen hissed another spell and, all at once, she was disguised as a very old pedlar woman.

She set off into the forest and at length came to the dwarfs' cottage. She knocked on the little door and called, "Apples for sale! Delicious, juicy, sweet apples!"

Snow-white thought it was rude to ignore the woman, so she put her head out of the window and said, "I'm afraid I can't let anyone in, the seven dwarfs have forbidden me to."

"Do not be afraid, I mean you no harm," said the old woman, smiling. "Look, I will eat some first. Then you will see that it is quite safe." The woman drew out a gleaming knife and sliced a big piece off the green half of the apple. She took a large bite into it. "See?" she said. "Lovely!"

Then Snow-white could no longer resist. She reached out through the window and took the rosy half. No sooner had she taken a bite than she fell down, dead. The disguised queen laughed a dreadful laugh and hurried back to the palace.

When the dwarfs came home and found Snow-white, they were horrified. They checked to see if she was breathing – but alas, she wasn't! They hugged each other and wept, and all the wild creatures that lived in the forest wept for lovely Snow-white too.

The dwarfs couldn't bear to bury the girl underground. Instead, they made a glass coffin and laid her in it. They wrote on it in golden letters: 'Here lies Snow-white, the princess.' They set it outside the cottage in a lovely spot and took turns watching over it, so Snow-white was never alone.

Days turned into weeks, and weeks turned into months, but very strangely, Snow-white never changed. She always looked as if she had just fallen asleep.

Then, one day, a king's son came riding through the forest and stopped at the dwarfs' cottage to rest. They sadly showed the prince the glass coffin in which the beautiful girl lay as though asleep.

As the prince gazed upon Snow-white, he fell deeply in love with her. As he leaned

closer to the coffin, he stumbled and bumped it. To everyone's astonishment Snow-white coughed. The piece of apple had been stuck in her throat and now came flying out! Snow-white opened her eyes and sat up.

The prince insisted on taking Snow-white back to his palace to recover. It wasn't long before the two were married, and the dwarfs were guests of honour at the wedding.

Meanwhile, Snow-white's stepmother was asking her mirror, "Mirror, mirror, on the wall, who is the fairest of them all?"

The magic mirror replied: "The new queen, Snow-white, is the fairest of them all."

The wicked woman began to burn with fury, so hotly that her magic set her on fire. Before long, she was just a pile of ashes, and she could never harm Snow-white again.

The Gold Children

There once lived a fisherman and his wife who were very poor. They lived in a tiny cottage. One day the fisherman caught a golden fish in his net.

"Put me back in the water and I will

change your cottage into a castle," the fish promised. So the fisherman put the golden fish back and went home to find a splendid castle standing where his tiny cottage once was. He went inside to find his astonished wife sitting at a table laid with a feast.

However, the couple's luck did not stop there. One day they noticed that outside the castle door, two golden lilies had sprouted. Then a horse in the stables gave birth to two

golden foals. Next, the fisherman's wife gave birth to two baby boys who were also made entirely of gold!

The children grew into tall, strong, handsome young men, and they were the best of friends. The time came when they said to the fisherman: "Father, we want to take our golden horses and ride away to explore the world. Watch the two golden lilies outside the door – if they are blooming, you will know that we are safe and well. If they start to fade, you will know that we are in danger or sick. And if the lilies die, you will know we are dead too." With that, they said goodbye and rode off down the path.

The brothers journeyed until they came to

an inn. The people all laughed and jeered when they saw the men made of gold. One of the brothers was so upset by the mocking that he turned round and went straight back home. However, the other decided to keep going. He covered himself and his horse with animal skins, so the gold could no longer be seen. Then he set out once more.

A little further down the road, he came to a village. He saw a girl there whom he thought was the most beautiful girl he had ever seen. He leapt off his horse, walked straight up to her and asked her to marry him. To his delight, even though he was still covered by his animal skins, she fell in love with him too and said yes. The wedding was

held that very same day, with much rejoicing.

That night, the young man dreamt he was hunting a splendid stag. It all seemed so real that when he woke up, he told his wife about it and set off into the forest, to see if it would come true.

It wasn't long before the young man glimpsed a fine stag through the trees, just as in his dream. He took aim with his bow and was about to shoot it when the stag ran away. The young man ran after it, over hedges and ditches, for a whole day without feeling tired. But by evening, he had lost the trail. He looked all around him, wondering which was the way out of the forest.

After walking for some time he noticed a

little house among the trees. He approached and knocked at the door, thinking he would ask for food and water. But when it opened, there stood a witch!

"What are you doing walking through the middle of the great forest so late at night?" the ugly old woman croaked.

"I have been hunting a stag," the young man explained.

"What? You've been trying to kill my stag!" the witch screeched. She pointed her finger and muttered some evil words and the young man fell to the ground and was transformed into a large rock. Then the witch laughed to herself and went back into her cottage and slammed the door.

All through the night the young man's bride waited for him, worrying that something terrible had happened, and in the morning he still had not returned.

Meanwhile, back at the fisherman's castle, the young man's brother noticed one of the golden lilies beginning to droop! "Good heavens!" he cried. "My brother must be in danger!" He sprang onto his golden horse and galloped down the road like the wind – away from his home… past the inn… and into the great forest.

There he found the little cottage and saw the huge stone lying outside – at once, he knew it must be his poor brother.

The witch heard him gasp and came

hobbling out of her house. "I've never seen a golden man before," she called. "Come here, my dear. Let me look at you." Of course, she wished to trap him!

But the young man did not go near her. Instead, he raised his bow and took aim and said: "I will shoot you, if you do not bring my brother to life again."

Then the witch snarled – but she had no choice. She touched the stone with her

The Gold Children

forefinger, and the young man immediately changed back to his human shape. He threw off his animal skins and leapt up behind his brother on his golden horse, which sprang away through the forest, like the wind. How the witch howled to see the two golden men escaping her clutches!

So the young man went back to his wife, who was overjoyed to have him back – and astonished to see him in his true golden form.

And when his brother returned back home, he found the drooping golden lily was standing tall and straight, blooming beautifully once more.

Then they all lived happily for the rest of their days.

The Valiant Little Tailor

One summer's morning a little tailor was sitting at his workbench by his window, cheerfully sewing. His tummy began rumbling so he took some bread out of his cupboard and spread a slice thickly with jam. "I'll just finish sewing that jacket before I take a bite," he said to himself. So he left the bread on a plate nearby while he sewed a few more stitches.

The sweet smell of the jam brought some flies buzzing in. "Shoo!" cried the tailor, waving his hand at them. "Go away!" But the flies wouldn't give up and kept zooming around the jam. The tailor grew annoyed and took off his shoe. *SLAM!* He brought it down on the table hard and when he lifted it there were seven dead flies underneath – seven!

"Look at that! I have killed seven creatures with one blow!" the tailor said to himself, admiring his own skill. He set the jacket to one side and quickly ran himself up a belt with the words embroidered on it: *SEVEN AT ONE BLOW*. 'When I wear this, everyone will read what I have done,' he thought with glee, and he locked up his little house and set off to spread the word of his brave deed around the world.

The tailor wandered down a road, always following his own pointed nose. After some time, he arrived at the courtyard of a royal palace. He felt weary, so he lay down on the grass and fell asleep. Some people walked by while he was dozing peacefully. One of them noticed the tailor's belt and read it aloud: "'*SEVEN AT ONE BLOW*'. Ah," he said to his companions, "he must be a mighty warrior." And they all hurried off to tell the king.

The king was delighted and ordered the tailor to be brought before him at once, for he had an important task to give him. "In a forest over the hill there are two giants who are terrorizing my people," the king told the tailor. "Every day the giants go out robbing and murdering people, and burning down their houses. If you can get rid of these two giants for me, I will give you my daughter's hand in marriage and half of my kingdom!"

'That would be a fine thing for a man like me!' thought the little tailor. "Great," he said boldly, "I will do that for you, no problem."

So the tailor set out and soon came to the forest of which the king had spoken. There were the two giants, sleeping under a tree,

snoring so that the branches waved up and down. The little tailor quickly and quietly gathered two pocketfuls of stones. Then he nimbly climbed the tree. He perched on a branch just above the sleeping giants and then threw down a stone onto the chest of one. Immediately the giant woke up and gave his friend a shove. "Hey! Why are you hitting me?" he yelled.

"You must be dreaming – I haven't touched you!" the other giant replied.

The pair settled back down to sleep. But as soon as the snoring had begun once more, the tailor threw a stone down onto the chest of the second giant.

"Why are *you* throwing things at *me*?" the

second giant roared, sitting up and pushing his friend awake.

"You must have gone mad," shouted the first giant, "I'm not throwing things at you!"

They argued for a while but they were both so weary that they closed their eyes again. Then the tailor picked the biggest stone out of his pocket and threw it with all his might on the first giant's chest.

"Now you're for it!" the first giant bellowed. He sprang up and punched his friend on the nose. The other hit him straight back – and so it went on, until at last they both fell down dead.

Then the little tailor leapt down from the tree and hurried back to tell the king the good

news. "It is done," he announced. "Now where is my reward?"

So the king, whether he liked it or not, had to keep his promise. And that is how a cheeky little tailor married a princess, won half a kingdom and became a king – all through swatting flies!

The Little Folks' Presents

Once upon a time, a tailor and a goldsmith were travelling together. One evening they heard beautiful music. They followed the sound to see where it was coming from.

Eventually, when the moon had risen, the tailor and the goldsmith reached a hill on which they saw a crowd of tiny men and women. They were holding hands, swinging round in a happy dance, and singing sweetly.

In the middle of the tiny people sat a tiny old man. He beckoned the tailor and goldsmith, inviting them to join the dance.

The little folk opened their circle and the two astonished men joined in.

As the dance whirled round, the old man took out a large knife. Before the tailor and the goldsmith knew what was happening, he seized them, one after the other, and in a flash shaved their heads bald! It all happened too quickly for the two men to be frightened. The old man clapped them on the back in a friendly manner, as if to say 'well done'. He pointed to a heap of coal nearby and signalled that the men were to fill their pockets.

The tailor and the goldsmith obeyed, although they did not know what use the coal would be to them, and off they went down the road once more.

The two travellers soon found an inn. Exhausted by their strange adventures, they sank into their beds and fell fast asleep.

In the morning, the tailor and the goldsmith were astonished to find that their hair had grown back, thicker than ever. They were even more delighted to discover that their pockets were filled not with lumps of coal, but with gold!

The two men were now rich – but the goldsmith was greedy. That evening, he left the tailor at the inn and hurried back to the hill. There were the tiny folk dancing, just as before. The old man again signalled for the goldsmith to join in, then shaved him bald and indicated that he should take some coal

away with him. The man stuffed his pockets and filled two bags that he had brought with him. Then, very pleased with himself, he set off back down the road to the inn.

Next morning, the goldsmith hurried to examine his pockets and bags. But to his surprise there wasn't any gold – only coal! How disappointed he was! "Oh well, at least I still have the first lot of gold I collected," he said to himself, and went to examine that. How shocked he was to find that this had turned back into coal too!

Just then, the goldsmith caught sight of himself in the mirror. Not only was he still bald, he now had a huge hump upon his back!

Then the goldsmith realized that he had

been punished for his
greediness, and he let
out a wail. The
tailor said kindly:
"Don't be upset,
I'll share my
riches with you."
And so he did.

But the greedy
goldsmith
never forgot
his mistake, for he stayed bald, with a hump
on his back, for the rest of his days.